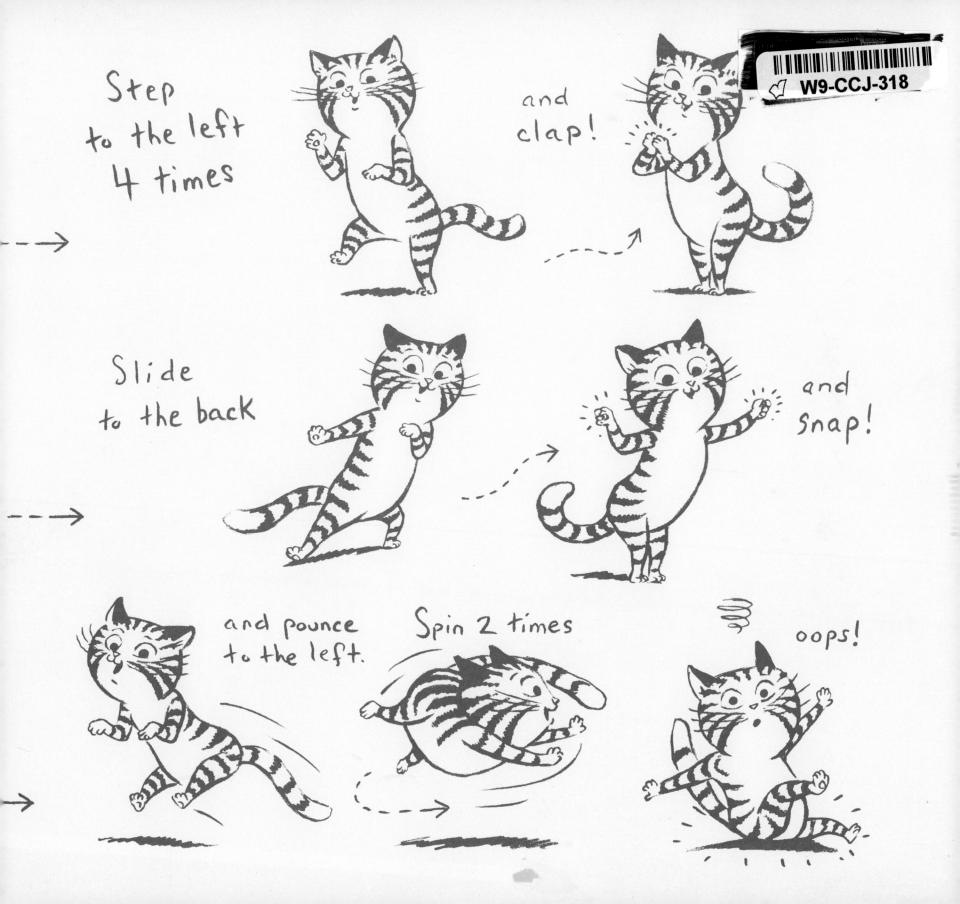

Little Lola
Saves the Show

By **Julie Saab**

Pictures by
David Gothard

Greenwillow Books
An Imprint of HarperCollins *Publishers*

Little Lola Saves the Show
Text copyright © 2016 by Julie Saab.
Illustrations copyright © 2016 by David Gothard.
All rights reserved. Manufactured in China.
For information address HarperCollins Children's Books,
a division of HarperCollins Publishers,
195 Broadway, New York, NY 10007.
www.harpercollinschildrens.com

Watercolors were used to prepare the full-color art.
The text type is 23-point Imperfect.

Library of Congress Cataloging-in-Publication Data
Saab, Julie.
Little Lola saves the show / by Julie Saab ;
pictures by David Gothard.
pages cm
"Greenwillow Books."
Summary: "While exploring, Lola the cat comes across
a stage with a ballet performance about to begin.
Lola puts on a costume and joins right in, dancing
beautiful pirouettes, arabesques, and pas de chats
(the step of the cat). When she accidentally stumbles
and trips, however, it is up to Lola to save the show"
—Provided by publisher.
ISBN 978-0-06-227453-3 (trade ed.)
[1. Ballet dancing—Fiction. 2. Cats—Fiction.]
I. Gothard, David, illustrator. II. Title.
PZ7.S112Lis 2016 [E]—dc23 2015014178

16 17 18 19 20 SCP 10 9 8 7 6 5 4 3 2 1
First Edition

 Greenwillow Books

This is Little Lola. She is off to a flying start.

Lola loves to stretch. This is her morning routine.

Downward dog,

twist,

fish pose,

cobra pose,

pigeon pose,

and cat pose (Lola's favorite).

Next, she skips, hops, and bops through the park!

Where are you going now, Little Lola?

Places, everyone!

The show is about to begin.

flamenco

Wait—
Lola wants to be
in the show, too.
But what can she be?

Irish
Step Dance

Jazz

Perfect!

Lola performs each step beautifully.

The plié,

pirouette,

and the pas de chat—
the step of the cat
(Lola's favorite).

sissonne,

arabesque,

Lola is a star!

Until . . . Look out!

BANG!

BUZZZZ . . .

Uh-oh,
Little Lola!

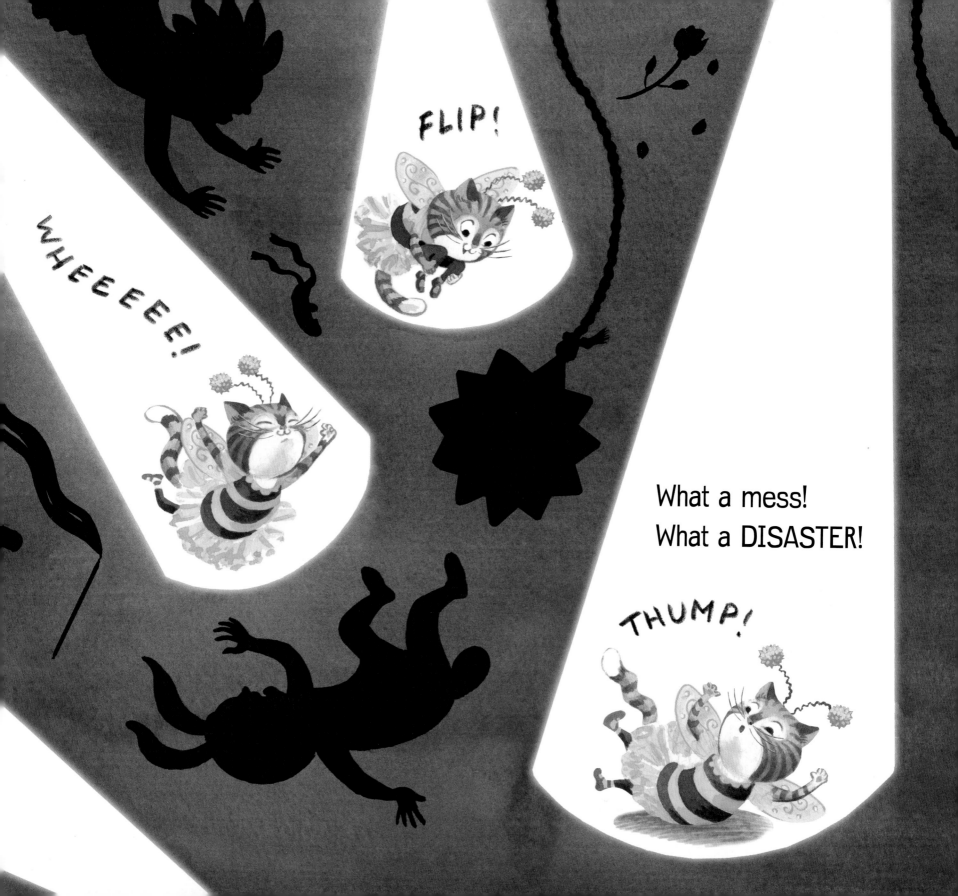

But not for long.

Lola turns on the lights,

sweeps up, patches up,

and fixes

and tidies
everything.

The show must go on.

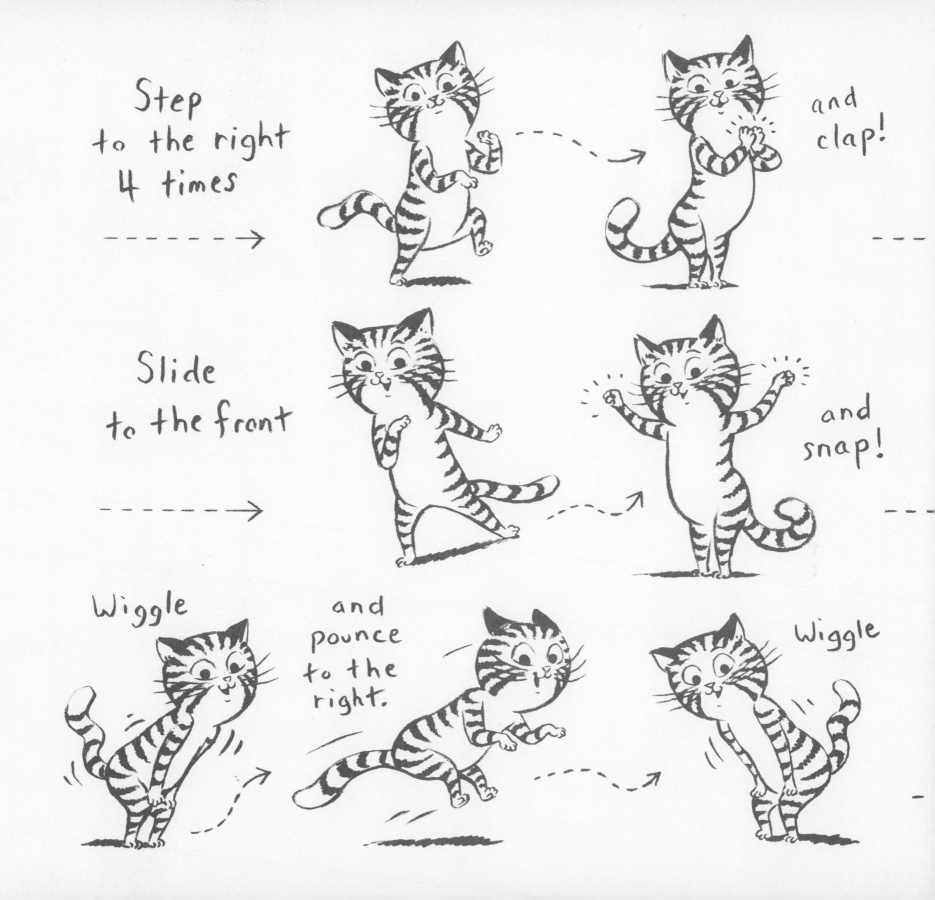

Step to the right 4 times ------->

and clap!

Slide to the front ------->

and snap!

Wiggle

and pounce to the right.

Wiggle

Good-bye, Little Lola. See you tomorrow.